Frank W. Dormer presents . . .

To Gus

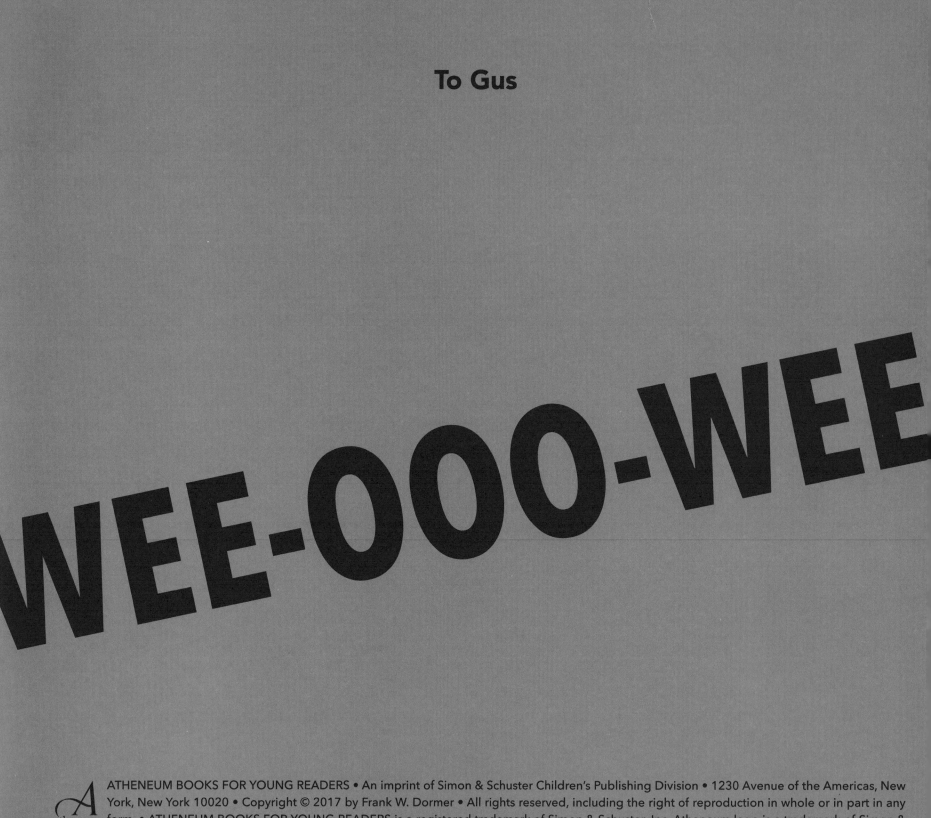

WEE-OOO-WEE

ATHENEUM BOOKS FOR YOUNG READERS • An imprint of Simon & Schuster Children's Publishing Division • 1230 Avenue of the Americas, New York, New York 10020 • Copyright © 2017 by Frank W. Dormer • All rights reserved, including the right of reproduction in whole or in part in any form. • ATHENEUM BOOKS FOR YOUNG READERS is a registered trademark of Simon & Schuster, Inc. Atheneum logo is a trademark of Simon & Schuster, Inc. • For information about special discounts for bulk purchases, please contact Simon & Schuster Special Sales at 1-866-506-1949 or business@simonandschuster.com. • The Simon & Schuster Speakers Bureau can bring authors to your live event. For more information or to book an event, contact the Simon & Schuster Speakers Bureau at 1-866-248-3049 or visit our website at www.simonspeakers.com. • Book design by Sonia Chaghatzbanian • The text for this book was set in Avenir Next. • The illustrations for this book were rendered digitally. • Manufactured in China • 0317 SCP • First Edition • 1 2 3 4 5 6 7 8 9 10 • Library of Congress Cataloging-in-Publication Data • Names: Dormer, Frank W., author, illustrator. • Title: Firefighter duckies! / words and pictures by Frank W. Dormer. • Description: First edition. • New York : Atheneum, [2017] • Summary: Firefighter Duckies fill a busy day with everything from rescuing a whale that is stuck in a tree to helping a monster who is having trouble seeing. • Identifiers: LCCN 2015051070 • ISBN 9781481460903 (hardcover) • ISBN 9781481460910 (eBook) • Subjects: • CYAC: Firefighters–Fiction. • Ducks–Fiction. • Rescue work–Fiction. • Animals–Fiction. • Humorous stories. • Classification: LCC PZ7.D7283 Fir 2017 • DDC [E]–dc23 • LC record available at https://lccn.loc.gov/2015051070

Here are the FIREFIGHTER DUCKIES!

Atheneum Books for Young Readers • New York London Toronto Sydney New Delhi

They are brave.

gorillas in chef hats!

They are the FIREFIGHTER DUCKIES!

They are brave.

They are strong.

They rescue . . .

whales in trees!

They are the FIREFIGHTER DUCKIES!

They are brave.

They are strong.
They rescue . . .

dinosaurs on bicycles!

And . . .

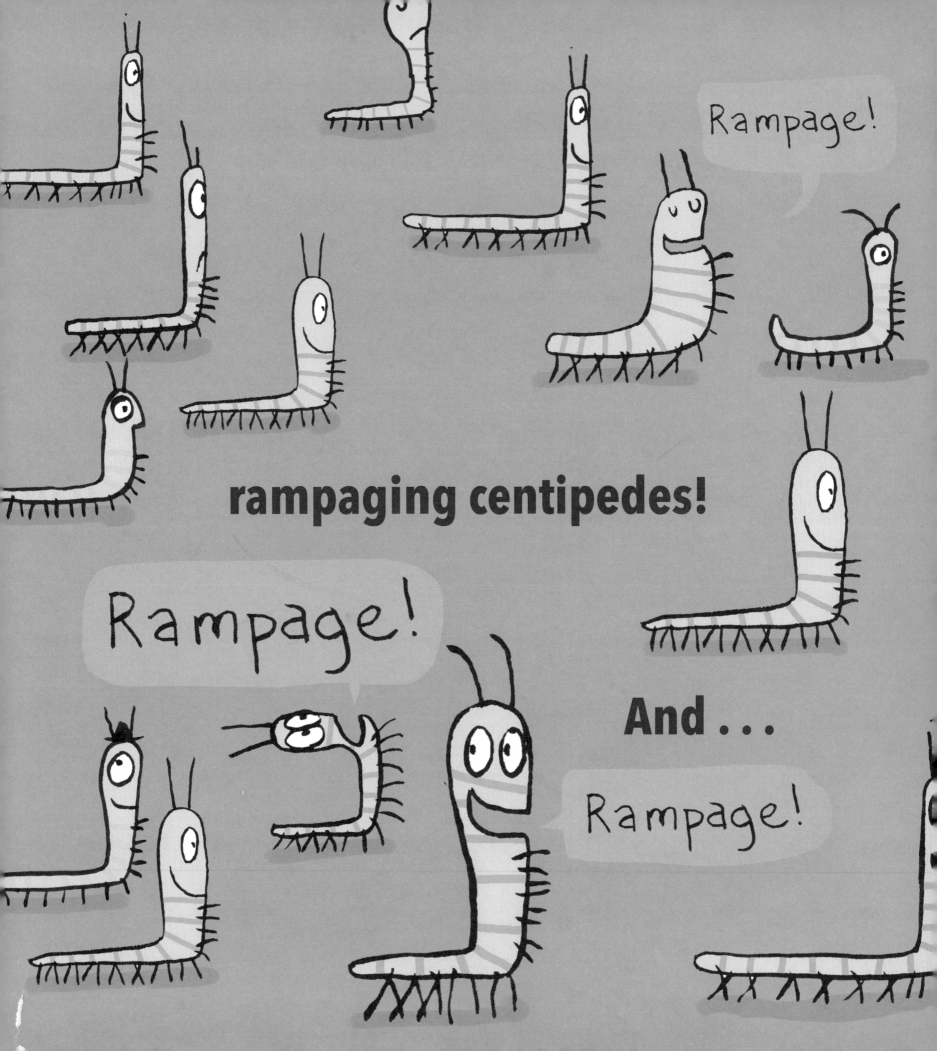

smushed-up lemurs!

And . . .

They
are
THE
FIREFIGHTER
DUCKIES!!!

They are
BRAVE.

They are STRONG.

They are . . . giving haircuts?

They are helpful.

They are kind.

They are the Firefighter Duckies.

They are brave.
They are strong.
They are helpful.
They are kind. . . .